KELI'S MAGIC STONE

WRITTEN AND ILLUSTRATED BY
MAMA ANNIE

ISBN   0-9637637-4-1

Every Sunday Keli went to see his grandma, Tutu. Tutu's little house sat in a beautiful garden, shaded by a huge mango tree. Keli loved Tutu's garden. He loved to pick mangos and bananas for lunch. He loved to chase the geckos from flower to flower. But most of all he loved to listen to Tutu's stories.

One day Tutu said,
"Oh look Keli, I've found a
magic stone for you."
Keli looked.
"It's very pretty Tutu, but
what's magic about it?"
"If you always keep this
stone with you, you will always
be happy. And when you are
happy, everyone around you
will be happy too."

Keli took the stone.
He could feel a big happy
smile spread across his face.
He ran home as fast as he could
to tell his Mom and Dad about
the stone.
"Mom! Dad! Look what Tutu
gave me. It's a magic stone
that makes me always happy."

"How wonderful," said Mom.
"Oh, that Tutu," said Dad.

The very next day,
while Keli was practicing his
death-defying trapeze act, a
mynah bird snatched up the
magic stone.

"Oh no," cried Keli, "Come back
with my stone."

But the mynah bird flew far out
of sight with Keli's stone.

Keli went straight to his best
friend Pueo, the owl.

"Pueo, my Tutu gave me a magic
stone to make me always happy
and the mynah bird stole it."
"Now, now, don't worry Keli,"
said Pueo," We will go find it. Mynah
probably didn't know it was yours."

Pueo took a very deep breath
and ruffled his feathers until
he was much larger. Then he said,
"Okay Keli, now climb on my back
and off we go."

Pueo flew Keli to the old Banyan tree in the middle of town where all the mynahs gathered.

"Ah, excuse me," he called, "Have any of you seen the mynah bird that took my stone?"

Well, Keli got lots of answers but they didn't do him much good.

Next they flew to the
top of the volcano to ask
Nene, the goose if she had
seen a mynah with a stone.
"Well, I certainly have a splendid
view from here and yes, yes I do
believe I saw a mynah, I believe he
was flying toward the rain forest."
So Keli and Pueo flew into the dark
and mysterious rain forest.

Keli looked around.
"Boy, if it's in here,
Pueo, I'm really in
trouble."

Keli and Pueo tried every secret place they could think of. They spotted a magic looking stone on a rock in the middle of the breakers. Keli was glad he'd been practicing his trapeze act but, too bad, it was the wrong stone.

Keli was getting very discouraged.
Pueo was sad for his little friend.
"I can only think of one place we
haven't looked," he said.

Pueo and Keli scoured the
coral gardens. They had so
much fun they almost forgot
the stone. They didn't find it.

Well, they had done their very best
and now they had to give up. Pueo
gently dropped Keli in his own backyard
and flew back to his home above the sugar
cane fields. Keli wasn't a bit happy now. In
fact, he was very sad. He knew he had to
go tell Tutu he had lost the magic stone. He
knew now he would never be happy again.

The next day was Sunday again but
Keli wasn't excited to see his grandmother.

Even his Mom and Dad felt sorry
for Keli but they knew he had to
go. And he did. He walked right up
to her and said,
"Tutu, I'm so sorry and you'll
probably be mad at me but I lost
the magic stone."
Then he told her about mynah and
Pueo and all the places they'd been.
Well! You'll never believe what Tutu
did.

She got the biggest smile
on her face that you ever
saw and then she swept
Keli up in a giant bear hug.
"First," she said, "I am never
going to be mad at you because
you're my wonderful Keli boy."
Then Tutu picked up a new stone
and said,
"This one will do just as well,
because the magic is,
If you think you're happy, you're
happy."

Now Keli did feel happy, really, really,
happy, but he kept the stone anyway,
just to remind himself.

"If I think I'm happy, I'm happy."

Andrea Cleall, the writer and illustrator of this book, has studied art and design all of her life. This is her fourth children's book, all of which reflect her love of the Pacific Island people and cultures. She is the mother of six and grandmother of two and is known as Mama Annie.

This book is for my children, especially Sean and Shiloh who taught me all about little boys.

Other books by Mama Annie:

Island Dancers coloring book
Island Adventures coloring book
Amazing Sea Creatures coloring book